THE BEGINNINGS OF DEMOCRACY

NICOLAS BRASCH

Australia • Brazil • Japan • Korea • Mexico • Singapore • Spain • United Kingdom • United States

The Beginnings of Democracy

Fast Forward
Purple Level 20

Text: Nicolas Brasch
Illustrations: Boris Silvestri
Editor: Johanna Rohan
Design: Stella Vassiliou
Series design: James Lowe
Production controller: Seona Galbally
Photo research: Michelle Cottrill
Audio recordings: Juliet Hill, Picture Start
Spoken by: Matthew King and Abbe Holmes

Acknowledgements
The author and publisher would like to acknowledge permission to reproduce material from the following sources: Photographs by Photographs by AAP Image/ Jim Baynes, p 23 top; The Art Archive, p 22/ Musée des Beaux Arts Troyes / Dagli Orti, p 21; Corbis/ Michael Maslan Historic Photographs, p 8; Getty Images, p 7/ AFP/ Attila Kisbenedek, p 6; Newsphotos, p. 4/ Guy Thayer, p 5; Photolibrary/ The Bridgeman Art Library, front cover, pp 1, 23 bottom/ The Print Collector, p 20/ Mary Evans Picture Library, p 9.

ISBN 978 0 17 012667 0
ISBN 978 0 17 012657 1 (set)

Cengage Learning Australia
Level 7, 80 Dorcas Street
South Melbourne, Victoria Australia 3205
Phone: 1300 790 853

Cengage Learning New Zealand
Unit 4B Rosedale Office Park
331 Rosedale Road, Albany, North Shore NZ 0632
Phone: 0508 635 766

For learning solutions, visit cengage.com.au

Printed in Australia by Ligare Pty Ltd
6 7 8 9 10 11 12 21 20 19 18 17

Evaluated in independent research by staff from the Department of Language, Literacy and Arts Education at the University of Melbourne.

Contents

Chapter 1

DEFINING DEMOCRACY

Democracy is a system of **government**. It involves members of a community having a say in the way they are governed.

However, the amount of involvement people can have in the way they are governed differs a lot.

A true democracy would give
every person in a community
the right to vote on every issue.
This form of democracy
would be difficult in practice,
because it would take too long for decisions
to be made.
It would only work well in a small community.

Today, a democracy usually involves people voting for others to **represent** them.

The **representatives** then make decisions on behalf of the community, instead of every member of a community voting on every issue.

This form of government is called a representative democracy.

Countries with a representative democracy include:

Tony Blair, Prime Minister of the United Kingdom

Chapter 2

THE ANCIENT GREEKS

The word democracy comes from the Greek language.

It is believed that the ancient Greeks were the first people to form **democratic societies** about 2600 years ago.

ancient Greec

The word democracy comes from the Greek words *demos*, which means 'the people', and *kratein*, which means 'to rule'. So the word democracy means 'rule by the people'.

Running Words 158

In ancient Greece, most states and communities were led by a single person or a small group of people. These people made all the decisions that affected the community.

But, the Greeks decided this system was unfair. So they thought up fairer ways for decisions to be made.

The ancient Greeks came up with a system of government where the country was split into small states.

All the male citizens in the states voted on important issues.

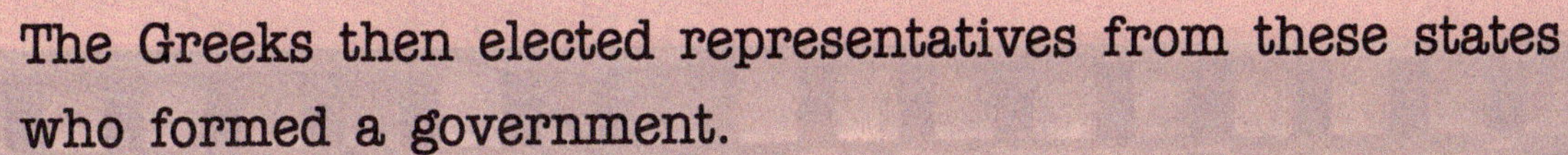

The Greeks then elected representatives from these states who formed a government.

The role of the representatives was to ensure that the decisions made by the citizens were carried out.

The representatives could not make their own laws.

This democratic system worked well in ancient Greece for two main reasons.

First, ancient Greece was quite small.

The ancient Greeks were able to create small states with no more than 10 000 people in them.

This made democratic decision-making possible.

Second, this system of democracy worked well in ancient Greece because the Greeks limited the type of people who could vote.

Women weren't allowed to have a say in decision-making.

Slaves weren't allowed to have a say in decision-making, either.

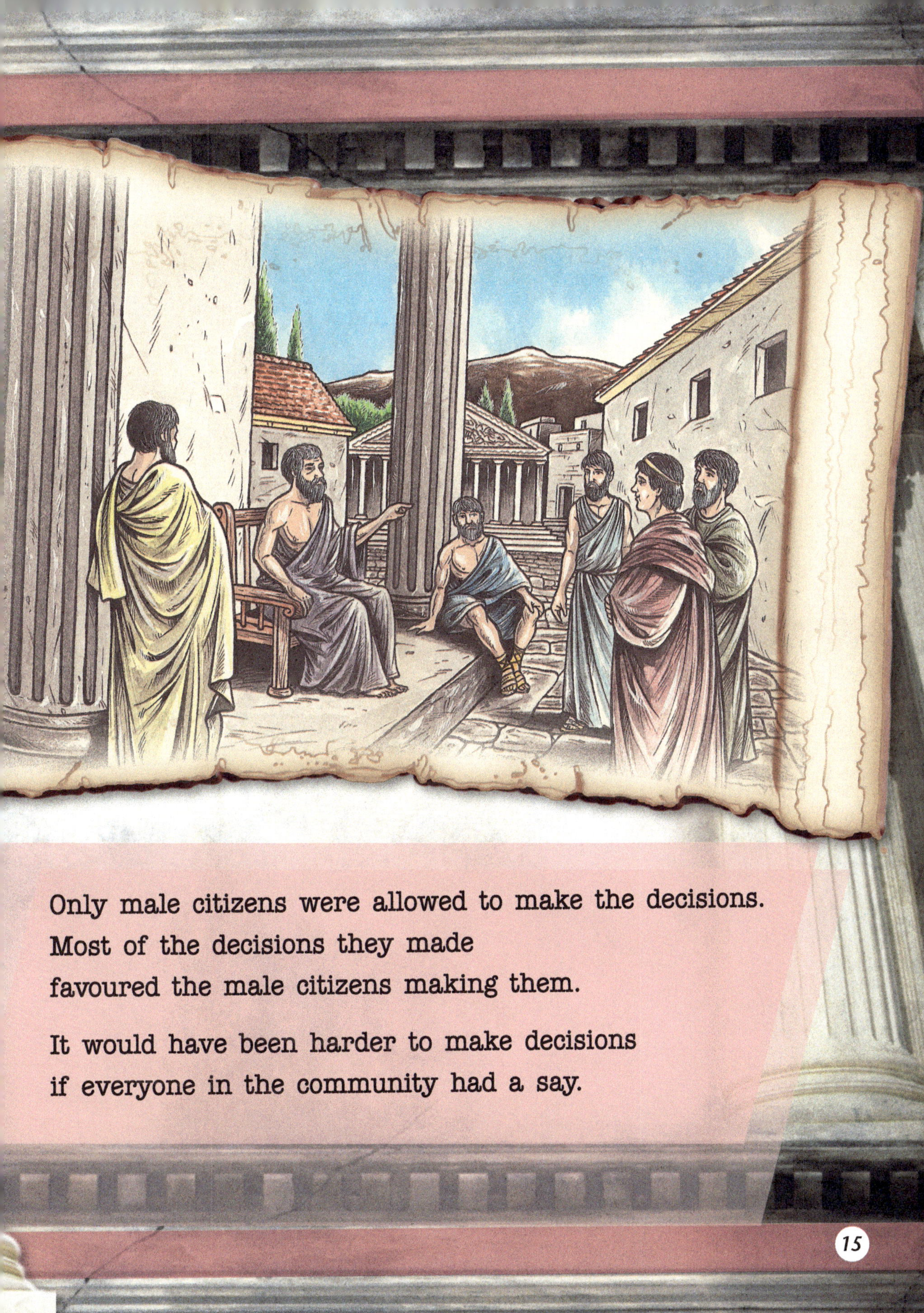

Only male citizens were allowed to make the decisions. Most of the decisions they made favoured the male citizens making them.

It would have been harder to make decisions if everyone in the community had a say.

Chapter 3

THE ANCIENT ROMANS

The ancient Romans took some aspects of Greek democracy and formed their own democratic systems.

Ancient Roman democracy was closer to modern representative democracy than the ancient Greek version.

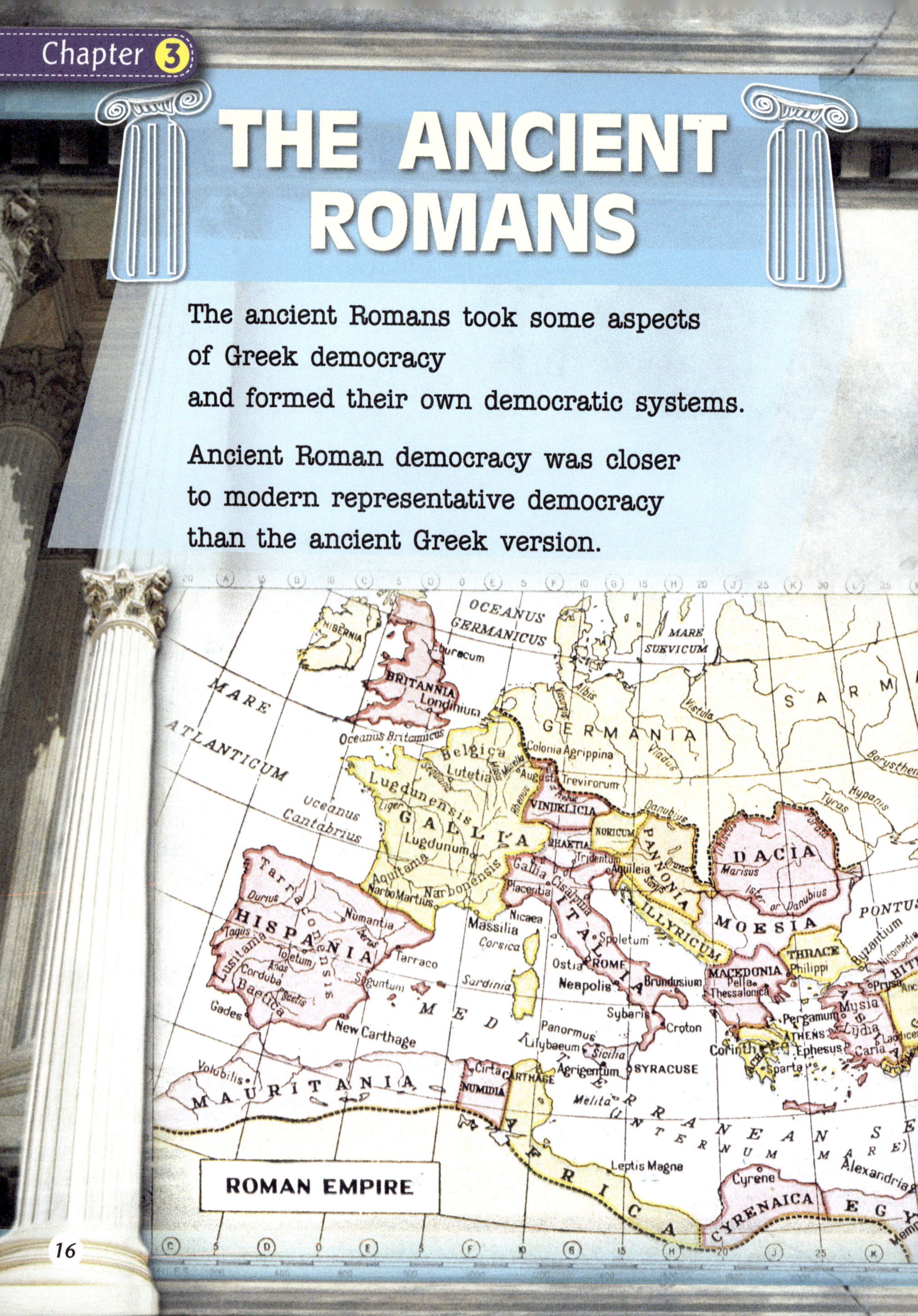

Instead of giving men the right to vote
on individual issues,
the Roman system allowed men to elect other men
to represent them in a government.

The elected representatives then made the decisions.

Like the Greek form of democracy, the Roman version only involved men.

In addition, wealthy men had more representatives in government than poor men.

So, most of the decisions made in ancient Rome favoured wealthy men.

Chapter 4

THE SPREAD OF DEMOCRACY

When the **Roman Empire** ended about 1600 years ago, democracy nearly ended as well.

Apart from a few small states in Europe, countries around the world were ruled by individuals or small groups.

Queen Elizabeth I (1533 - 1603)

For the next 1200 years,
not much changed.

But, by the 1600s,
the people in several European countries
started to rise up against their leaders.

the French people rise up against Édouard Molé, cardinal of Bayeux, in 1648

In 1649, King Charles I of England became the first major ruler in Europe to be overthrown. He was tried for **treason**, found guilty and beheaded.

The execution of King Charles I led to the formation of an English government based on democratic ideas.

Other European countries followed, including France.

However, these new democratic nations didn't extend the idea of democracy to the countries they **colonised**.

These colonies had to fight for their own democratic governments. In some cases, they fought until the end of the 20th century.

Independence day celebrations in the Solomon Islands

the House of Commons, England, 19th century

Glossary

colonised	set up control over a foreign land
democratic societies	communities supporting and embracing democracy
government	the ruling body of a country or state
represent	to act or speak for people
representatives	people chosen to act or speak for other people
Roman Empire	the empire under Roman rule, from 27 BC to 395 AD
treason	the crime of betraying your country

Index